"This upbeat series really encourages the very young to 'go for it!' with bright vocabulary, illustration and concept . . . These lovely books are true boosters for preschool confidence, self-concept and beginning reading skills."

—*School Library Journal*

Bear takes a walk all by himself and is very brave as he climbs tall mountains, crosses high bridges, and even frightens away some flying dragons! But he's very glad to see Daddy walking by when he gets stuck on the edge of a cliff. And crossing the busy street is definitely better with Daddy by his side. Bear's active imagination makes his walk exciting, but his common sense keeps him out of trouble.

This book offers encouragement to small children who, like Bear, are just beginning to test their independence, but who must also learn to stay within reasonable limits.

SHIGEO WATANABE is the author of many outstanding books for young people, and has also translated many of the world's great children's books into Japanese. Acclaimed illustrator YASUO OHTOMO brings to this book the warmth, simplicity and humor for which he is especially known. Both he and Mr. Watanabe live near Tokyo, Japan.

I Can Do It All By Myself
books by
Shigeo Watanabe

How do I put it on?
AN AMERICAN LIBRARY ASSOCIATION
NOTABLE CHILDREN'S BOOK
What a good lunch!
Get set! Go!
I'm the king of the castle!
I can ride it!
Where's my daddy?
I can build a house!
I can take a walk!

an I CAN DO IT ALL BY MYSELF book

I can take a walk!

Story by Shigeo Watanabe Pictures by Yasuo Ohtomo

PHILOMEL BOOKS

I can take a walk all by myself!

I'll just slip
through the fence.

I can climb this tall mountain.

I can cross this high bridge.

Boo!

I really scared
those flying dragons!

Now I'll cross this deep river.

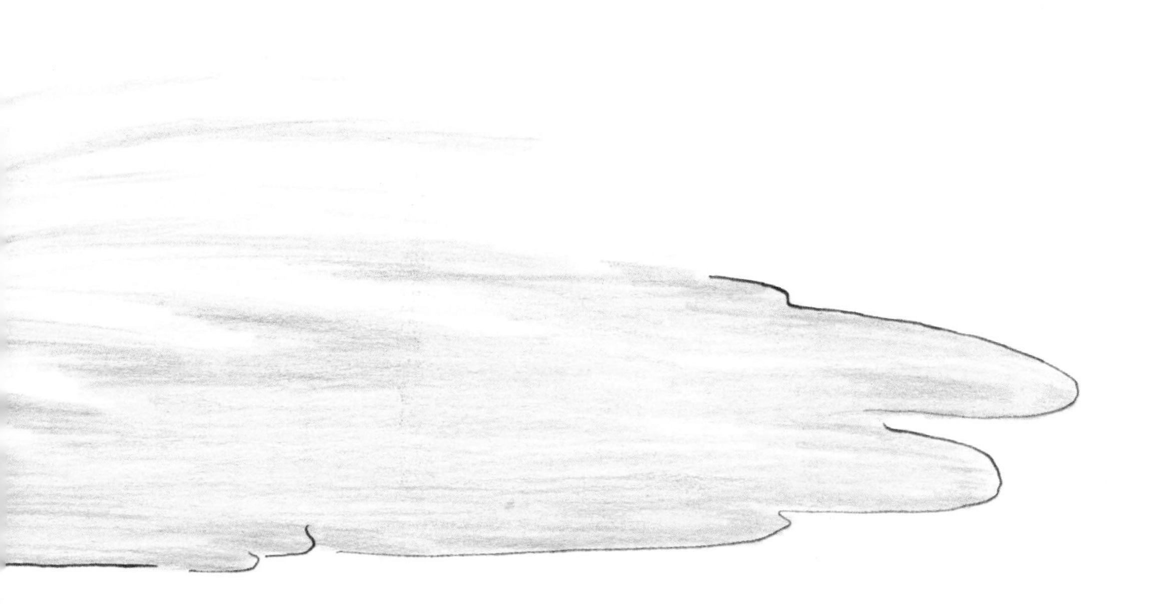

I can climb along th

edge of this high cliff.

Oops! Now how will I get down?

Daddy!
I'm so glad to see you!
Let's walk home together.

Wait!
The light is red.
We can't cross
the street yet.

Now it's green.
Let's go!

What a good walk!

a division of The Putnam & Grosset Book Group
200 Madison Avenue, New York, NY 10016
Originally published by Fukuinkan-Shoten, Tokyo, 1983
Printed in Hong Kong
Library of Congress Cataloging-in-Publication Data
Watanabe, Shigeo   I can take a walk!
Translation of Itte Kimasu!
Summary: Taking a walk all by himself, a young bear
is glad to have his father join him on the way home.
(1. Walking—Fiction.   2. Bears—Fiction)
1. Otomo, Yasuo, ill.   II. Title.
pZ&.W26151cb   1984   (e)   83-17397
ISBN 0-399-21848-3 (GB)
ISBN 0-399-21847-5 (pbk)
First GB Edition (revised)
First Paperback Edition (revised)